MAY 9 6

DATE DUE	
OCT 2 0 1998	OCT 2 0 2000
NOV 2 8 1998	MAR 3 1 2001
FEB 0 3 1999	JUN 1 3 2001
FEB 1 7 1999	AUG 2 1 2001
	OCT 1 3 2001
	JAN 2 0 2002
MAR 1 8 1999	SEP 0 9 2002
APR 1 3 1999	
	JUN 0 9 2004
MAY 0 4 1999	
	JUN 3 0 2004
JUL 2 8 1999	JUL 2 7 2004
AUG 1 3 1999	
	JUL 1 5 2005
SEP 1 7 1999	
NOV 0 2 1999	MAR 2 4 2006
MAY 0 2 2000	
JUN 1 3 2000	
AUG 0 8 2000	
GAYLORD	PRINTED IN U.S.A.

I DON'T WANT TO GO TO CAMP

BY EVE BUNTING

ILLUSTRATED BY MARYANN COCCA-LEFFLER

BOYDS MILLS PRESS

Published by Caroline House
Boyds Mills Press, Inc.
A Highlights Company
815 Church Street
Honesdale, Pennsylvania 18431
Printed in Mexico

Publisher Cataloging-in-Publication Data
Bunting, Eve.
    I don't want to go to camp / by Eve Bunting ; illustrated by
Maryann Cocca-Leffler.—1st ed.
[32]p. : col. ill. ; cm.
Summary : A young girl is convinced she does not want to go to camp
until her mom enrolls in a camp for mothers only.
ISBN 1-56397-393-6
1. Camps—Fiction—Juvenile literature. 2. Family life—Fiction—Juvenile
literature. [1. Camps—Fiction. 2. Family life—Fiction.]
I. Cocca-Leffler, Maryann, ill. II. Title.
    [E]—dc20   1996   AC
Library of Congress Catalog Card Number 95-75747

First edition, 1996
Book designed by Tim Gillner and Maryann Cocca-Leffler
The text of this book is set in 15-point Palatino.
The illustrations are done in gouache and colored pencil.

10 9 8 7 6 5 4 3 2

To Lael—You and I love summer camp
      —Eve

To Diane, Rosanne, Ann,
Laura, and Karen, who along
with me would love to go to a
mother's camp
    Love, Maryann

Lin was having a tea party with Loppy Lamb when Mom came into the kitchen.

Mom waved a letter. "I'm going to camp," she said happily.

"Only kids go to camp," Lin said.

Mom shook her head. "This is a mother's camp, for mothers only."

Lin poured Mom a cup of pretend tea. "Loppy Lamb and I don't want to go to kid's camp."

"Of course not," Mom said. "Anyway, you're both too little. You couldn't go to any kind of camp for two years."

"We don't want to go in two years," Lin said. "We've decided."

"Of course," Mom said.
She got a pad of paper and
began making a list.
"Would you and Loppy Lamb
like to come shopping with me?"

"Sure," Lin said.

Mom bought a lot of things.

"I didn't know you got
a big red flashlight,
and a blue sleeping bag
with a rainbow on it,
and a yellow duffel
when you went to camp," Lin said.
"But we still don't want to go to camp."

"Of course not," Mom said.

She bought a harmonica, too.
When she blew into it a great blast
of sound came out.

The other shoppers held on to
their hair.

"Does everyone who goes to camp
get a harmonica to blow in?"
Lin asked.

"Sure," Mom said.

"We still don't want to go,"
Lin said.

Mom gave her a hug.
"Of course not."

Two weeks later, Dad and Lin and Loppy Lamb drove Mom to the camp bus. Lin had never seen so many moms in a bus before.

"Bye!" the mothers called as the bus rolled away.

"Bye!" the dads and kids called back.

"Don't forget to come see us on Visitors Day," the moms yelled.

"We won't," the dads and kids yelled back.

Lin held Loppy Lamb close to her ear. "Loppy Lamb says not to be sad. Mom will be home in six days."

"He's right," Dad said. "Besides, it's good for moms to be with other moms sometimes. And for dads to be with their little girls."

"And for little girls to be with their Loppy Lambs," Lin added.

On Tuesday Dad said,
"Tomorrow is Visitors Day.
Let's make some treats to
bring to Mom."

They baked cookies.

They made fudge.

"I didn't know you got butterscotch
cookies and chocolate fudge on
Visitors Day," Lin said.

Dad sampled a cookie.
"That's part of the fun."

The next day they drove up
the winding camp road.
They saw squirrels, crows,
and a dinosaur.
Only Lin and Loppy Lamb
saw the dinosaur.
Lin told Loppy not
to be scared.

"It's only an *Apatosaurus*,"
she said. "Some people still
call them *Brontosauruses*.
But *Apatosaurus* is the right name.
They don't eat little lambs
or little girls."

Mom came running to meet them.

She wore a baseball cap.

She had a scab on each knee.

After she hugged them she said,
"Come see my cabin."

The cabin had four bunks.

"We're all moms and all best friends,"
Mom said. "We have our own password
and a secret code. Our cabin won
the canoe race. But Sunflower
cabin beat us at volleyball."

Lin gasped.
Canoe races! Volleyball!

Mom opened the treat boxes
and passed them around.
"Yum! Butterscotch cookies
and chocolate fudge.
I'll have to save some for
tonight's midnight feast.
But it's all right.
You brought lots."

"You have midnight feasts
and best friends
and passwords
and secret codes
and canoe races
and volleyball games at camp?"
Lin asked.

"Sure," Mom said.
"Have another piece
of fudge."

There were horses to
ride that afternoon.

There was a lake to swim in.

A girl named Valerie had
a swimsuit just like Lin's.

Some of the kids swung over
the water on a tree branch,
but Lin didn't.

"Loppy Lamb's afraid
I might fall,"
she explained to Valerie.

After dinner they sat around
a campfire and made
marshmallow mushies.

Lin and Valerie traded friendship
bracelets. Valerie said she couldn't
wait till she was old enough
to go to camp. She said she would
go when she was seven.
She didn't want to wait till
she was a mother.

Lin didn't say anything.

The night was sparkly with stars
when Mom walked them back
to their car.

"Don't you get homesick?"
Lin asked.

"We all do. But then we talk about
how soon we'll be back with our
families and how much fun we're
having. I take out my harmonica
and play *Good Golly, Miss Molly*.
We all sing. Oh, Lin! We are
so loud!"

Mom giggled and
Lin giggled, too.

"Give me a good-bye hug
till Saturday," Mom said.
She hugged Lin and Dad
and then said,
"You, too,
Loppy Lamb."

Lin looked back as the car pulled away.

Mom was waving.

Lin could see the campfire and the tall, beautiful trees.

"Dad?" Lin said.
"Loppy Lamb wants to tell me something."
She held him close to her ear. "Really?" she asked. "*Really?*"

"Dad? Loppy says he might want to go to camp in two years when he's big. He says it looks like fun. He says he'll need a big red flashlight, and a blue sleeping bag with a rainbow on it, and a yellow duffel, and a harmonica that he can blow in."

Dad patted one of Loppy's long ears. "That can be arranged."

They were coming to the
Apatosaurus place. Lin tucked
Loppy Lamb's head under her
jacket so that he wouldn't see.
"He gets scared," she whispered
to Dad. "He's such a baby sometimes.
I might *have* to go to camp with him."

"That would be nice," Dad said.
"You take such good care of your
Loppy Lamb."

Lin nodded.
"It's not that I *want* to go."

"Of course not," Dad said.